Please ask an adult to help you.

1. Carefully cut around the edge of the bracelet following the dotted line. Then cut along the three short dotted lines.
2. With the pattern on the outside, bring the two straight ends towards each other.
3. Ask an adult to slot the ends together.
4. Now your sparkly bracelet is ready to wear!

Princess Ponies

A Dream Come True

With special thanks to Julie Sykes

Bloomsbury Publishing, London, New Delhi, New York and Sydney

First published in Great Britain in March 2013 by Bloomsbury Publishing Plc
50 Bedford Square, London WC1B 3DP

A CIP catalogue record for this book is available from the British Library

ISBN 978 1 4088 2728 4

Typeset by Hewer Text UK Ltd, Edinburgh
Printed and bound in Great Britain by CPI Group (UK) Ltd, Croydon CR0 4YY

1 3 5 7 9 10 8 6 4 2

www.bloomsbury.com
www.ChloeRyder.com

Princess Ponies

A Dream Come True

CHLOE RYDER

BLOOMSBURY

LONDON NEW DELHI NEW YORK SYDNEY

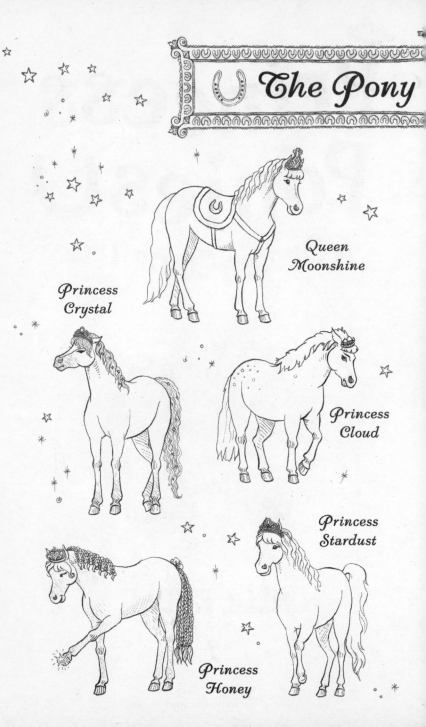

The Pony

Queen
Moonshine

Princess
Crystal

Princess
Cloud

Princess
Stardust

Princess
Honey

Royal Family

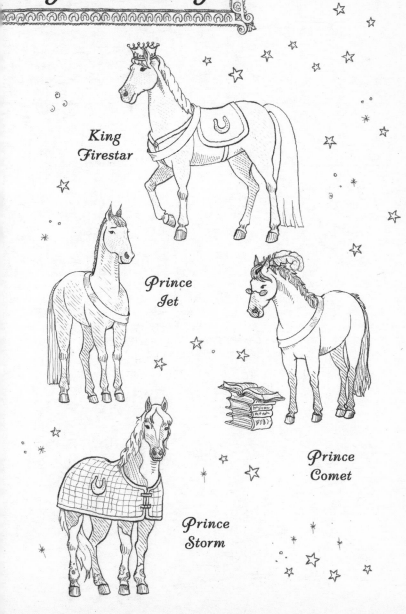

King
Firestar

Prince
Jet

Prince
Comet

Prince
Storm

Chevalia

Horseshoe Hills

Savannah

Grasslands

SAND SCHOOL

Canter's Prep School

Plateau

Mane Street

Early one morning, just before dawn, two ponies stood in an ancient court-yard, looking sadly at a bare stone wall.

'In all my life this wall has never been empty. I can't believe that the horse-shoes have been taken – and just before Midsummer Day too,' said the stallion.

He was a handsome animal – a copper-coloured pony, with strong legs and bright eyes, dressed in a royal red sash.

The mare was a dainty yet majestic palomino with a golden coat and a pure white tail that fell to the ground like a waterfall.

She whinnied softly. 'We have so little time to find them all.'

With growing sadness the two ponies watched the night fade away and the sun rise. When the first ray of sunlight spread into the courtyard it lit up the wall, showing the imprints where the golden horseshoes should have been hanging.

'Midsummer Day is the longest day of the year,' said the stallion quietly. 'It's the time when our ancient horseshoes must renew their magical energy. If the horseshoes are still missing in eight days, then by nightfall on the eighth day, their magic will fade and our beautiful island will be no more.'

Sighing heavily, he touched his nose to his Queen's.

'Only a miracle can save us now,' he said.

The Queen dipped her head regally, the diamonds on her crown sparkling in the early morning light.

'Have faith,' she said gently. 'I sense that a miracle is coming.'

Chapter 1

Pippa MacDonald blinked sleepily and stared around the unfamiliar room. For a moment she didn't know where she was. She remembered going on holiday to the seaside with her family, but this wasn't their holiday home. The bed next to hers was huge, with a straw duvet and a horseshoe-shaped headboard decorated with rosettes. And fast asleep in the big bed was a pony – a Princess Pony!

All at once Pippa's memory flooded back. She *had* been on holiday, until two enormous seahorses had whisked her away to the island of Chevalia, a magical world inhabited by talking ponies, where no human had ever set foot before. Time existed in a bubble there, and Pippa wouldn't be missed at home, for no time was passing in her own world.

There she'd met Princess Stardust, and learnt that Chevalia was in grave danger. Eight golden, magical horse-shoes used to hang on an ancient wall in the Castle courtyard. Once a year, on Midsummer Day, the horseshoes' energy was renewed by the sun. But the horse-shoes were missing, and if they weren't returned by Midsummer Day then Chevalia would be no more.

Pippa had been amazed to learn that she'd been brought to Chevalia to find the magical horseshoes. Yesterday, after a long, exciting and dangerous search, she and her new friend, Princess Stardust, had rescued one horseshoe from the foothills of the spooky Volcano. But there were still seven more to find and there were only five days left until Midsummer.

Quickly, Pippa got up and looked for her clothes. She'd hung them on a chair the night before but now in their place was a new outfit — a white top patterned with pink and blue horseshoes, a smart pair of pink jodhpurs and some matching sandals. Thrilled, Pippa put the new clothes on, then borrowed one of Stardust's combs to untangle her dark, curly hair.

Stardust was still fast asleep.

'Wake up, lazy hooves,' Pippa said, gently shaking her.

Princess Stardust opened her eyes, yawned and closed them again.

'There's no time for sleeping in,' said Pippa. 'Chevalia is still in danger.'

'I was having the most wonderful dream,' mumbled Stardust. 'I had a pet girl.' Her eyes flew open and she sat up. 'It was true!' she exclaimed. 'I really do have a . . .'

Pippa scowled and crossed her arms over her chest.

'I mean, a new special friend,' said Stardust hurriedly. 'Today's a very special day – we should get ready.'

Stardust went to her dressing table and combed her long, white mane. Then Pippa placed Stardust's pink jewelled tiara on to her head, between her ears. Pippa smiled as she adjusted the sparkling tiara into place.

'Let's get going then,' Stardust said excitedly.

Stardust's room was at the top of the eighth turret in Stableside Castle. They hurried down the tower's spiral ramp to the ground floor and were just heading towards the dining room for breakfast when Stardust's big sister, Princess Crystal, appeared, going in the opposite direction.

Crystal had an apricot-coloured coat with an inky black mane and tail and a white blaze running down her face. She was extremely pretty and spent many hours making sure she looked her best.

'Hurry up,' she whinnied impatiently. 'There's a family meeting in the courtyard.'

'A family meeting about what?' Pippa whispered to Stardust.

'We're always having family meetings,' she said vaguely. 'I'm starving – are you? What about breakfast?' she called after Crystal.

'You should have thought about that when you were sleeping in. It's a good thing you're not going to be Queen one day.' With that, Crystal trotted ahead, towards the courtyard.

Pippa put her hand on Stardust's side.

'Don't mind her,' she said. 'Big sisters just don't understand.'

'She still treats me like I'm a foal,' said Stardust.

'She may have a bigger tiara,' Pippa said, smiling, 'but you have a girl for a best friend.'

'Yes, I have,' Stardust said, smiling back and following her sister.

Reaching the wooden door that opened on to the courtyard, Crystal stopped and turned around. 'It's Royal Family only,' she said haughtily. 'Your pet should wait here.'

'Pippa's my best friend and she's here to save Chevalia,' said Stardust. 'That makes her the same as family!'

Crystal rolled her eyes. 'You exhaust me,' she neighed, leading the way.

Stardust and Pippa joined the Royal

Ponies gathered in the courtyard. Crystal and Prince Jet stood to attention, nudging each other for the best position to greet their mum and dad. Prince Comet had his nose buried in a book. Honey was doing twirls to show off her glittery new hoof polish, while Cloud was mumbling grumpily. Prince Storm strode in last, covered in mud, causing Crystal to snort crossly.

'Storm, you could have washed. You look like you just trotted off the farm!'

'I did,' he replied. 'The fields won't plough themselves.'

'Stop bickering, children,' chided Mrs Steeplechase, the royal nanny. She pushed the Royal Ponies into an orderly line, ready to welcome the King and

Queen. 'I trust you've all had breakfast and are ready for the Royal Games?'

Pippa's stomach rumbled noisily as she looked at Stardust in alarm.

'Games?' she asked. 'But I thought we were going to search for the missing horseshoes?'

'Was that your stomach, Princess Stardust?' Mrs Steeplechase tutted crossly. Dipping her head inside her satchel, she brought out a shiny red apple and tossed it to Stardust, who deftly caught it in her mouth. She threw another apple to Pippa.

'Thank you,' Stardust and Pippa said.

'Hmmph!' snorted Mrs Steeplechase. 'Just don't be late for breakfast again.'

Pippa stared at the stone wall, where one lonely golden horseshoe sparkled in the sunlight. There were still seven empty spaces left to fill. Suddenly she didn't feel so hungry any more.

Stardust followed Pippa's gaze to the Whispering Wall.

'The Royal Games are very important –' she started, but she was interrupted as the Queen and King trotted regally into the courtyard.

As one the Royal Ponies straightened up, with their ears held forward. Bowing their heads, they whinnied, 'Good morning, Mother. Good morning, Father.'

The Queen looked up at the wall and then turned to address her children. 'The annual Royal Games are taking place today and, although Chevalia is in danger, it's important that we keep up with our traditions. The whole island will be looking to us for how to behave. If we panic about the missing horseshoes, then everyone will panic. Do you understand?'

The Royal Ponies nodded and chorused, 'Yes, Mother.'

'Stardust,' Pippa whispered, 'if the Royal Games are so important then maybe I should look for the horseshoes on my own?'

'Don't do that,' said Stardust. 'You'll miss out on the fun. There are so many great events – dressage, showjumping, horseshoe-tossing, polo, and the Equestriathon race around the entire island!'

'The Games do sound amazing,' said Pippa.

'They take place on the Plateau,' explained Stardust, 'on the far side of Mane Street. It's not too far from the beaches, so we can search them afterwards.'

'OK,' Pippa said, feeling a little happier that Stardust wasn't completely forgetting about the horseshoes. 'We'll stick together.'

'Like best friends,' said Stardust.

'Like best friends,' Pippa agreed, stroking Stardust's long, soft mane.

Queen Moonshine whispered something into her husband's ear then turned and nodded at Pippa.

Pippa flushed and her stomach did a cartwheel. She could guess what the Queen had said. The Royal Ponies and the ponies of Chevalia were depending on her.

'We *will* find the missing horseshoes,' Pippa said determinedly.

Chapter 2

Queen Moonshine lined her family up in age order. Princess Crystal was first, perfectly groomed and dressed in her best tiara, looking every bit the Queen-in-training. She was followed by her three brothers and three sisters, with Stardust, the youngest Royal Pony, at the end.

'What a fuss,' Storm said quietly. 'I don't know why I have to go to the

Royal Games when there's so much to do on the farm before the harvest.'

'But the polo team needs you,' said Stardust. 'You're their best player.'

'Do you play polo, Stardust?' asked Pippa.

'I wish I could play but Mrs Steeple-chase won't let me. She says I'm too young.' She sighed crossly. 'The only game they let me play is horseshoe-tossing, which is for babies.'

The King and Queen led the Royal Family from Stableside Castle to the Plateau at a smart trot. Pippa was glad that Mrs Steeplechase had allowed her to ride on Stardust's back or she might not have kept up. Pippa looked out for the missing horseshoes as she rode towards the Royal Games grounds. Away to her left was the Wild Forest. She was surprised to see that three ponies were gathered by the edge of the trees. The largest, a stocky pony, was cloaked in a dark grey coat and hood, with a few strands of chestnut mane showing. There was something familiar about it.

'Stardust,' Pippa whispered urgently, 'who's that over there by the Wild Forest?'

'Where?' asked Stardust.

'Right there,' Pippa said, pointing. But when she looked again, the ponies had disappeared into the woods.

'Was it the wild ponies? They're brilliant fun. I wish I was allowed to play with them,' Stardust said wistfully.

Pippa fell silent. They hadn't looked like wild ponies and Pippa was sure she'd seen the large, hooded animal before. If only she could remember where.

As they approached the Royal Games grounds, the delicious smells of warm bran mash and steamed carrot juice drifted towards Pippa. An enormous horseshoe arch marked the entrance. It was decorated with red, blue, yellow, green, pink and purple rosettes, and their silk ribbons fluttered colourfully in the light breeze. One by one, the Royal Family ducked under the horseshoe arch, to the rapturous hoof-stamping of the hundreds of gathered ponies. The Queen led them into the royal box, which was higher than the rest of the audience and gave an excellent view of the entire show ring.

Conscious that the whole crowd could see her, Pippa carefully slid off Stardust's back. There was a loud crackle followed by a shrill whinny, then a deep voice sounded over the tannoy system.

'Ponies and foals, please show your appreciation for the arrival of Their Majesties Queen Moonshine, King Fire-star, the Prince and Princess Ponies: Crystal, Jet, Cloud, Honey, Comet, Storm and – not forgetting the little foal of the family – Stardust. Plus our very special guest Pippa MacDonald.'

There was a thunderous roar and the ground shook with even more stamping. Pippa's face felt hot and her chest tightened as she stared shyly at the enormous crowd. She'd never seen so many ponies all in one place. There was every kind, from tiny Shetlands with shaggy manes covering their eyes to magnificent thoroughbreds with highly polished coats.

'Mmm, can you smell that carrot juice?' said Stardust. 'I could drink a whole trough of it.'

'You're only hungry because you slept through breakfast,' Cloud said irritably.

'I could drink a troughful of carrot juice too,' said Honey. 'Let's go and get some together. Do you like my hooves by the way? I wasn't sure which colour to paint them.'

'I *love* your hooves,' said Stardust.

'They are pretty,' Pippa said, taking in Honey's glittery pink-and-purple-striped hooves.

'Where did you get the polish from?' asked Stardust.

'The Mane Street Salon. Excuse me!' Honey said indignantly, as Crystal and Jet pushed past to get to the front of the royal box.

'Out of my way, Jet. The crowds are here to see me,' said Crystal.

'No, they're not,' Jet said, winking at a group of young fillies and grinning when they blushed. 'It's me they've come for.'

'Well, they're certainly not here for me,' Storm said, grinning at Pippa.

'I'm not surprised,' Crystal said moodily. 'You might have cleaned up your hooves at least, Storm, if you're going to stand in the royal box.'

'Don't worry, Storm,' Stardust whispered. 'No one's interested in me either.'

Pippa sighed. Stardust seemed to have forgotten they had an important job to do.

'I'm going to start looking for the horseshoes,' Pippa said impatiently.

'Wait for me! Sorry, Honey, I've got to go,' added Stardust. She hurried after Pippa, stepping out of the royal box and into the crowd.

'We'll never find anything here. There are too many ponies around!' Pippa said in despair. Then she thought of something. 'Do you think the crowd would help us?'

'That's a great idea!' said Stardust.

Stardust's enthusiasm was infectious and she soon had a group of eager ponies helping her to search the showground. Pippa tried asking for their help too but many of the ponies just gaped at her in awe. They had never seen a real, live girl before. In the end she gave up asking and searched alone, keeping her head down to avoid all the curious stares.

The dressage competition started and many of the ponies lost interest in searching for the horseshoes and trotted over to the arena to watch. The Royal Family were settled in their box, enjoying the Games. Honey had a large bag of roasted pony-nuts that Stardust kept looking at longingly.

'Let's go and watch the dressage for a bit,' she said at last, when she couldn't resist any longer.

'We can't,' said Pippa. 'There are only five days left until Midsummer.'

Stardust nuzzled her nose in Pippa's dark, curly hair.

'I know,' she said softly. 'But you heard what Mum said about the Royal Ponies needing to carry on as normal. Let's search for a bit longer and then we really have to go and watch some of the events.'

Among the trees at the edge of the showground was a temporary stable block for the competitors. It was packed with ponies combing their manes and painting their hooves. Sashes and tail bandages fluttered from the trees and there was a strong smell of hoof oil.

A flash of light caught Pippa's eye. It was coming from a hollow in a wizened old tree. Something shiny was hidden inside. Her heart quickened as she went towards it and pulled it out.

'It's just a hoof pick,' she said, her shoulders sagging with disappointment.

'That's my lucky hoof pick!' said an excited voice. 'At least, I hope it's lucky.'

Pippa turned around to see a solid, chestnut pony, with a neatly plaited mane tied with blue ribbons, trotting up behind her.

'Blossom!' Stardust whinnied, blowing through her nostrils at the pony.

Blossom blew back, giggling as they touched noses.

'Are you competing in the junior dressage?' asked Stardust.

'I can't get out of it,' Blossom said sadly. 'You will come and watch me, won't you? Pleeeeease! I know I'll mess it all up if my best friend isn't there to cheer me on.'

'I'll try,' Stardust said casually. 'But

Pippa and I are busy right now. Pippa's here to find the missing horseshoes and I'm helping her.'

A hurt look crossed Blossom's face, but she swallowed and said bravely, 'I know. Everyone's talking about her – a real, live girl here on Chevalia.'

'She's my best pet ever,' Stardust said proudly.

Pippa rolled her eyes and cleared her throat, hoping that Stardust would remember that she wasn't a pet.

'I mean, Pippa's my best friend,' Stardust said hastily, realising her mistake.

Pippa noticed that Blossom's big brown eyes glittered with tears.

'B-b-best friend?' she stuttered. 'I thought I was your best friend.'

'You are. Well, you were until Pippa arrived,' Stardust said, unaware of Blossom's distress. 'Pippa's my best friend now, but you can be my second best.'

Just then the announcer called for the start of the junior dressage competition.

'Listen – they're calling your class,' said Stardust. 'You'd better go.'

'So are you coming to watch me?'

'I'm sorry, Blossom, but Pippa and I –'

'We'd love to watch,' Pippa interrupted. 'We'll both cheer you on!'

Pippa felt very uncomfortable as

they followed Blossom to the competition arena. It was obvious to her that she was upset, but Stardust didn't seem to have noticed.

'Blossom's too clumsy to be any good at dressage,' Stardust whispered. 'It's a shame, because she comes from a family of show ponies.'

When it was Blossom's turn to perform she trotted stiffly into the ring. Her hooves were all over the place and she kept tripping up.

Cinders, an unkind pony who was always quick to criticise others, was in the box below the royal one. She laughed as Blossom stumbled around the ring.

'Blossom's got four left hooves,'

she whinnied. Some of the other ponies laughed and snorted with her.

That only made Blossom worse. She trotted around the show arena like a circus clown. She finished with a wonky curtsy and hurried from the ring in tears.

'What's wrong with her?' asked Stardust. 'She always does badly in dressage, so why is she crying about it now?'

'Blossom's crying because you said she wasn't your best friend any more,' Pippa said quietly.

'That's silly!' Stardust exclaimed in disbelief. 'We can still be friends, but how can I have two best ones?'

'Very easily,' said Pippa. 'It's good to

have lots of friends. Imagine how you'd feel if I suddenly said I wanted to be Blossom's best friend and not yours.'

Stardust's face fell. 'I thought you liked me!'

'I do but that doesn't mean I can't like anyone else. I've got another best friend at home.'

'But you like me at the same time?'

Pippa nodded.

'Oh, I see,' Stardust said slowly. 'You *can* have two best friends.'

Now the junior dressage was over, Pippa wanted to continue searching for the missing horseshoes but she hated seeing Blossom so upset, especially when it was partly her fault. She decided to hide her impatience because she knew they had something to do first.

'Let's go after Blossom and tell her she can be your best friend too,' Pippa said.

Stardust hesitated. Pippa climbed on to her back and stroked Stardust's mane.

'Having two best friends will be twice as much fun,' Pippa said persuasively.

'OK,' said Stardust. 'I will have two best friends. Let's go and tell Blossom.'

Chapter 3

At first Stardust and Pippa couldn't find Blossom. They searched everywhere, including the competitors' area, but there was no trace of her. Then Stardust spotted her on the far edge of the showground.

'Blossom's going the wrong way!' she said. 'That path leads down to the beach.'

'She's fast!' Pippa exclaimed, watching Blossom gallop into the distance.

Blossom was also very fit. She galloped all the way down the path and didn't stop until she reached the beach. Stardust was hot and panting heavily by the time they caught up with her. Blossom stood staring out to sea with the surf swirling around her legs.

'Hi, Blossom,' Stardust said breathlessly. 'You can still be my best friend if you want. Pippa says I can have two.'

Pippa slid from Stardust's back and glared at her. 'Say sorry,' she mouthed silently.

Stardust tossed her head as if she might argue but Pippa kept glaring at her.

42

'I'm sorry,' she said at last. 'I didn't mean to hurt your feelings.'

'Really?' Blossom continued to gaze at the sea.

'Yes,' Stardust said, giving her a friendly nudge with her nose.

Finally, Blossom turned round. 'So we're still friends?' she asked.

'*Best friends*,' said Stardust. 'It's going to be twice as much fun having two best friends.'

'Can I be friends too?' Pippa asked, looking at Blossom.

'Yes! A real, live girl for a friend would be amazing,' said Blossom. 'I'm sorry I ran away. I was upset and when Cinders laughed at my awful dressage performance it was the last straw. I try so hard but I always trip over my hooves.'

'You're brilliant at galloping,' Pippa said kindly. 'You should enter the Equestriathon.'

'I'd love to, but Mum and Dad think that racing is for any old pony, not show ponies like us.' Blossom sighed.

'Traditionally Blossom's family have always been prize show ponies on Chevalia,' added Stardust. 'She can't just decide to be a racing pony.'

'But we can't all be good at the same things,' said Pippa. 'My mum says you should do the things that make you happy.'

'Well . . .' Blossom said hesitantly. 'I do love to gallop – it's my favourite thing. Well, that and being Stardust's best friend.'

'Pippa's right,' said Stardust. 'You should do the things that make you happy. And even if you don't win the trophy, every pony that completes the race gets a medal. But I'm sure you *can* win!'

Blossom fell silent for a while, then she said decisively, 'I'll do it. I'll race the Equestriathon. And if I win the trophy, hopefully Mum and Dad will be so proud of me they won't mind about the dressage. Will you come and support me?'

'Of course,' said Stardust.

Pippa bit back her frustration. She couldn't hurt Blossom's feelings by refusing, but she feared that at this rate they'd never find the missing horseshoes.

'Thank you.' Blossom's eyes sparkled happily. 'And one more thing, now that we're all best friends – can Pippa ride me in the Equestriathon? Pleeeeeaase! You know how much I've always wanted to carry a girl.'

'That's a brilliant idea, isn't it, Pippa?' said Stardust.

Pippa hesitated. 'Won't you run faster without me, though?' she asked.

Blossom's bottom lip quivered.

Pippa couldn't bear seeing her upset again, so she quickly added, 'How about I just ride you to the start line?'

'That would be wonderful! Thank you, Pippa. We'd better get going. I need to warm up on the practice gallops.'

As Blossom and Stardust trotted back up the beach, Pippa trailed behind, kicking up lumps of seaweed and checking behind rocks for the missing horseshoes.

When they reached the path towards

the Plateau, she turned back for one last look. Something caught her eye away in the distance. Pippa squinted out to sea and her heart missed a beat. It was Rosella and Triton, the two giant seahorses who had brought her to Chevalia. She wondered if they would be able to help. Pippa ran straight back to the water's edge, waving to get their attention. Gracefully, the seahorses changed direction and swam towards her.

'Hello, Pippa,' Rosella called.

'Is there a problem?' asked Triton, a green seahorse with dark freckles.

'Yes,' Pippa said breathlessly. 'Princess Stardust and I have only found one of the golden horseshoes.'

'Only one?' exclaimed Rosella. Pippa noticed that the seahorses gave each other disappointed looks.

'We brought you here, Pippa, because you are the girl who loves ponies the most,' said Triton. 'We hoped you could save Chevalia.'

Pippa felt awful. 'I won't let you

down,' she promised, 'but I could use your help.'

'What help do you need?' asked Rosella.

'Could you swim around the island and look at the places we can't see or reach from the land, like the rocks?'

'If there are horseshoes on the cliffs or in the rocks under water, we'll find them,' said Triton.

'Thank you,' Pippa said gratefully.

Proudly dipping their heads, they swam back out to sea.

Pippa raced to catch up with Stardust and Blossom. The two ponies were so busy talking about how Blossom should compete in the Equestriathon that they hadn't even noticed she'd been gone.

While Blossom warmed up for the race on the practice gallops, Pippa searched the scrubby ground either side of the race track for horseshoes. She wasn't surprised when she didn't find them, though – it was too open and flat to hide anything there.

At last it was time to ride Blossom over to the Equestriathon start line on the beach. A long blue ribbon marked the start of the race and a huge crowd had gathered all along the track. As Blossom approached it, proudly carrying Pippa on her back, the ponies began to whisper and stare. Pippa's face burned with embarrassment when she realised they were talking about her.

'Carrying a girl is cheating,' said a large pony with a narrow face.

'It's not fair on the others,' agreed an elderly black and white pony.

Pippa was very glad when Blossom reached her position on the start line. Sliding from her back, she stood close to Stardust, hoping the Princess Pony could protect her from the hostile looks. Once she was off Blossom's back, though, everyone returned their attention to the competitors.

'Good luck, Blossom!' Stardust shouted, earning herself a cross glare from Mrs Steeplechase, who was also in the crowd. 'Once you've started we'll go to the headland to watch the rest of the race.'

'Thank you,' Blossom said, looking pleased. 'I couldn't do this alone.'

King Firestar stepped forward. 'One hoof, two hooves, GO!' he called, striking a horseshoe-shaped gong.

The blue start-line ribbon fell to the ground. In a thunder of hooves and flying turf, the competitors galloped away. Blossom kept pace with even the biggest and most powerful of the racing ponies.

'Quick, Pippa,' said Stardust. 'Jump on my back so we can get to the headland faster. It's the best place to watch from because you can see at least half of the race from there.'

As soon as Pippa had swung herself on to Stardust's back, the pony set off at a gallop across the Plateau. The wind blew in Pippa's face, catching her curly hair so that it streamed out behind her. She felt her anxieties slowly melt away. This was exhilarating – the most fantastic ride in her whole life. She wanted to gallop for ever. Leaning forward, she sunk her hands deep in Stardust's soft, white mane.

'Faster,' she cried.

Stardust snorted. 'Hold on tight then,' she called, thrusting onward.

Pippa could tell that Stardust was enjoying the ride too. Her ears were pricked forward and she galloped with a joyous spring in her stride.

Pippa was so happy she almost shouted out loud. She felt so alive – and confident that everything would work out. Blossom would win the race, she was sure of it.

Chapter 4

They reached the headland quickly and Stardust stopped a safe distance from the cliff edge, her sides heaving as she caught her breath.

Pippa looked around. From this point, over half the island's white beaches were spread out below her. The island was ringed by deep-blue sea that sparkled like thousands of tiny jewels. It was so quiet up here that she could hear the soft hiss as the waves crept up the shore. But the beaches were a long way down and it gave her a sudden shiver to be up so high. She clung on to Stardust's mane and Stardust gently moved back two steps from the edge, sensing Pippa's nervousness.

'That's much better,' said Pippa. 'Chevalia's the most beautiful island ever, but it's very, very high up in places!'

Pippa looked down the stretch of beach to watch the ponies racing across the sand. Even though they were so tiny from this height, it was still possible to pick them out. White sand sprayed from their hooves as they thundered along. The stocky chestnut in the lead was Blossom. In second place, and a long way behind, was a skewbald pony, his neck stretched and steam rising from his body as he struggled to catch up. Next there was a tight cluster of four ponies who were bumping and jostling each other as they fought to overtake. The rest of the racers were spread out behind, with a group of stragglers bringing up the rear.

'Look – Blossom's so far ahead of the pack!' said Pippa.

'No one can catch her now,' Stardust whinnied. 'I'm sure she'll win.'

Excitement fizzed in Pippa's stomach. She couldn't wait to see Cinders's face when Blossom won the Equestriathon trophy. And what would Blossom's parents say? They might be show ponies but Pippa felt sure they'd be thrilled and proud of their daughter.

'You can do it, Blossom!' Pippa called.

Stardust joined in, chanting, 'Blossom, Blossom, Blossom!'

She trotted on the spot, bouncing Pippa up and down. It was so much fun that at first Pippa didn't notice that something was moving out at sea. Faster and faster, two shapes were swimming towards the shore, where they started dancing in the water. That got Pippa's attention. She put her hand up to shield her eyes from the sun.

'The seahorses are back,' she gasped.

But what were they doing? Suddenly, Pippa realised that they must want to speak to her.

'Who are you waving at?' Stardust asked, as Pippa threw both arms in the air.

'Rosella and Triton,' Pippa answered,

sliding from Stardust's back. 'They're calling me.'

'I'll take you down to the path to the beach,' said Stardust.

Pippa hesitated. Riding Stardust would be much quicker than going by foot, but what about Blossom? They had promised to watch her race.

'Thanks, but you'd better stay here. If Blossom gallops past when we're on our way down the cliff path, she won't see you cheering her on and she'll be so disappointed.'

'You're right,' Stardust said with a big sigh. 'Why does being a best friend have to be so difficult sometimes?'

'I don't know,' said Pippa. She climbed down from Stardust's back and, stroking her softly on the nose, added, 'But it's worth it.'

'Definitely,' Stardust agreed, nudging Pippa's hand.

'I won't be long. With any luck, I'll be back for the end of the race.'

Pippa set off at a run, haring across the headland as if she were racing in the Equestriathon herself. The ground was bumpy and covered in long, spiky grass that whipped against her legs. She gritted her teeth and ignored it. She ran so fast, and with her head down, that she almost missed the path. Pulling up sharply, Pippa turned left and stumbled down the steep track. Stones rattled under her feet, and once she slipped and nearly fell. Throwing her arms out to save herself, she flushed hot with panic. Luckily, she regained her balance and carried on, more slowly this time.

Far away, the seahorses watched, bobbing up and down in the water so urgently that Pippa thought this must be an emergency. The path turned abruptly, catching Pippa totally unawares and causing her to trip up. One minute she was running, the next she was pitching head first down the path. She was so shocked that her heart skipped a beat. Instinctively, she curled into a ball. She tumbled to the ground, hitting the path with a dull thud and rolling a short distance, until she stopped.

'Ouch!'

Now her heart was banging like a crazy drum. Everything ached. Gingerly, Pippa sat up and tested her arms and legs. She was amazed and relieved to discover that nothing was broken. Dusting the dirt and grit from her clothes, she took several deep breaths to steady herself then stood up slowly.

Out at sea the seahorses seemed to be still now. Pippa waved to show that she wasn't hurt. But as she started off again something pinged against her ankle. Stopping, she stared at her foot.

'No!' Pippa said in dismay.

The strap of her sandal had snapped, leaving the shoe hanging uselessly off her foot. Pippa stared at it for a moment then quickly tied the broken ends together. The strap wasn't long enough and kept coming undone. In desperation, she pulled a crumpled tissue from her pocket and wound it around the broken strap like a bandage. But as soon as she took a step the tissue fell away. Crossly, Pippa pulled the sandal off. Now what was she going to do?

Chapter 5

There was only one solution. Unbuckling the other sandal, Pippa slid it off then, holding a shoe in each hand, she bravely set off again. Dust oozed between her toes and tiny stones bit into her feet. Pippa ran on, wincing with pain and hobbling each time she stood on a really sharp stone. She was much slower without shoes, but she continued down the winding cliff path as fast as she could. She just hoped the seahorses would wait for her.

At last, the path flattened out and she could see the beach ahead. With an extra spurt of speed, Pippa ran on to the white sand, squealing with delight at its welcome softness. Faster now, she hurtled across the beach and splashed into the sea. The water was deliciously cold and soothing for her aching feet. She waded out until the sea reached her knees.

The seahorses met her, their enormous, curved tails brushing the seabed. Dipping their heads, they each touched their noses against Pippa's.

'Well done,' Rosella said, her eyes sparkling proudly.

'You were very brave just now,' added Triton, his voice gentle and deep.

Pippa flushed. She didn't feel brave — more annoyed that she'd fallen and broken her shoe.

'Have you found something?' she asked.

'I believe we have,' said Triton.

Pippa's heart leapt with joy then instantly plummeted as she could tell from the seahorses' anxious faces that it wasn't all good news.

'Is it a horseshoe?' she asked.

'We think so,' said Rosella. 'Something shiny and glittery is wedged in the rocks at the end of that jut of land. Can you see it?'

Pippa stared into the distance. She could see the rocks – three of them, with jagged tops and steep sides – but that was all. She took a step sideways and saw something flash.

'Yes,' she said, her voice rising with excitement. 'There's definitely something sparkly between the middle and end rocks.'

'You'll have to hurry,' warned Triton. 'The tide has turned and very soon those rocks will be under water.'

'Once the sea comes in it will be too late,' added Rosella. 'There's a nasty whirlpool around those rocks. It's very dangerous. Even with our magic we're not strong enough to get close to them.'

Pippa sized up the rocks. They were so far away and the sea was rapidly creeping up them. Suddenly she felt very small and alone. Could she really do this by herself?

'I must!' she said forcefully.

Pippa rushed along the beach. The sand was soft under her bare feet but running down the path from the headland had taken more out of her than she'd realised. The muscles in her legs ached with every step. She could feel herself slowing and, no matter how hard she tried, she couldn't make her legs work any faster. She was conscious of the water bubbling up the beach, its frothy white fingers curling around the rocks. What if the tide beat her and the whirlpool prised the golden horseshoe free and whisked it out to sea?

'No!' she panted. She couldn't let that happen. All eight of the golden horseshoes had to be in place on the Whispering Wall in time for Midsummer Day so that their magical energy could be renewed and Chevalia could be kept safe.

There was such a long way to go. It seemed hopeless, but Pippa didn't give up. On she ran, her heart pounding loudly in her ears, blotting out all other sounds. It was only when a shadow fell over her that she realised she wasn't alone.

'Stardust!' she squealed.

'You'd been gone such a long time I was starting to worry. I had to come and check you were OK. Get on my back,' Stardust called, slowing to a walk.

'I'm so happy to see you!' exclaimed Pippa.

'Well, what are best friends for?'

Pippa stumbled alongside her. Her legs were trembling and she didn't think she had enough energy to jump on to Stardust's back. Stardust seemed to realise this because she stopped and knelt down on her forelegs.

'I hope Mrs Steeplechase isn't watching right now!' she joked.

Pippa couldn't help laughing too. The royal nanny was so strict she wouldn't care if all seven of the missing horseshoes were in danger of being swept out to sea – manners and behaving like a proper Princess Pony came first!

Climbing astride Stardust's back, Pippa sunk her hands into her silky mane and wound it around them.

'Comfortable?'

'Very,' said Pippa.

She lurched sideways as Stardust rose up, only just remembering to squeeze her legs into Stardust's flanks to prevent herself from sliding over the pony's head.

'Let's go,' Stardust called, bucking with excitement as she raced away.

Pippa leaned forward like a jockey, taking some of her weight from

Stardust's back as they galloped across the beach. Sand sprayed up from Stardust's hooves and her long, white tail streamed behind her like a silky banner.

Was it her imagination or was the sea coming in even faster now? Pippa couldn't take her eyes off it as she willed it to slow down. It was no good. The sea closed in, licking against the bottom of the rocks and becoming deeper and deeper, until it spun round them in circles, like water whirling round a plughole.

'Faster!' Pippa cried urgently.

She threw herself flat against Stardust's neck, making herself as streamlined as possible. Stardust galloped harder, her breath coming in noisy rasps. Gradually, the rocks came closer, but poor Stardust was exhausted. As she lost speed, Pippa could hardly bear to watch the sea's greedy, blue fingers reaching up the rocks to the glittering object wedged there.

Bravely, Stardust galloped on but her stride was shorter and she kept stumbling. Now they were closer there was no doubt that the glittering object was a golden horseshoe. But there was still some distance to go to reach it. A white wave lapped over the horseshoe.

'Oh no!' groaned Pippa.

They'd finally found the second horseshoe but any second now they were about to lose it again.

Chapter 6

A pony was thundering up behind them, neighing loudly. Was it Mrs Steeple-chase? Pippa could hardly bear to look. But no, surely the royal nanny was too large to gallop that fast. Turning her head, she saw that it was Blossom.

'Blossom!' exclaimed Pippa. 'What are you doing here?'

'When the racecourse turned a corner I saw you both from the cliff top.

You promised you'd watch me and I knew you wouldn't let me down, so I guessed something must be wrong if you were down here on the beach. What's happened?'

'We've found one of the golden horseshoes,' Pippa said, pointing at the distant rocks. 'But it's almost under water!'

'You won't get there in time to retrieve it,' Blossom said, galloping beside Stardust. 'I'll go for you.'

Relief swept through Pippa but it was quickly replaced with despair.

'What about the race? You were in the lead.'

'I pulled out. Chevalia matters far more than the race.' Blossom snorted.

'Besides, winning isn't everything. Helping your friends is much more important.'

'But how will you get the horseshoe off the rocks?'

'With my hooves,' Blossom said bravely.

Pippa shook her head. The whirlpool was already too strong. Blossom would need all four hooves on the ground to withstand its force.

'I'll come with you,' she declared.

'There isn't time to stop for you,' called Blossom, who was starting to pull ahead of Stardust.

If Blossom was making sacrifices and putting herself in danger then Pippa must too.

'You don't have to stop. Come closer and I'll jump on your back,' she shouted.

'Pippa, no!' shouted Stardust. 'It's too dangerous. And you're scared of heights.'

But Pippa was too busy concentrating to answer. As Blossom moved closer she noticed that she was taller than Stardust. Could she manage to transfer herself from one pony to the other without falling off? With a shudder, she ignored the pounding sound of Stardust and Blossom's hooves.

Blossom matched her pace to Stardust's until she was exactly alongside her, then she closed the gap between them.

'Ready?' Blossom called.

Pippa swallowed hard. She felt light-headed suddenly but there was no time to lose. She reached out for Blossom's mane. It was still plaited from the dressage competition so there was little for her to hold on to. And how did she think she was going to get her legs over? Pippa realised that she would have to get into a crouching position to transfer herself from Stardust to Blossom's back. Pippa stared at the ground tearing by. It seemed a very long way down.

I can't do it, said a scared little voice inside her head. But Pippa had already done so much on Chevalia that she'd never thought possible. Gathering all her courage, she held tightly on to

Stardust's mane. She decided she would do it on the count of three.

One, two and . . . three.

Slowly, she leaned forward and brought her feet up behind her, on to Stardust's back. Seeing the ground moving so fast beneath her made her feel a little bit sick. Pippa refused to think about that. She fixed her gaze on Stardust's mane as she got her feet in the right position. Her heart was racing in time with Stardust's hoof beats and her mouth was dry. Pippa took a long, deep breath. She pushed herself up so she was crouching on Stardust's back. Now all she had to do was to jump over to Blossom. Pippa reached out for Blossom's plaited mane.

'I'm ready,' she called.

'Be careful,' shouted Stardust.

Pippa hesitated. Her head was spinning.

'Are you sure about this?' called Stardust.

Pippa didn't answer. She summoned up every last bit of courage – and leapt!

Her stomach dipped. She seemed to hang in the air for ever but it was only a few seconds before she landed with a bump on the other pony's back. Blossom was broader than Stardust and had a much bouncier stride. Pippa was flung up and down for a moment then, losing her balance, slid sideways.

'Help!' she squeaked.

Pippa hung on, her legs gripping more tightly around Blossom's sides. Blossom misunderstood this movement and, thinking that Pippa was asking her to go faster, she sped up. Lurching forward, Pippa desperately clung to Blossom's unravelling plaits. She couldn't fall off now – there wasn't time! She hauled herself to the middle of Blossom's back. She knew that she had been very lucky that nothing had gone wrong so far. Now that she had regained her balance, Pippa leaned forward and urged Blossom on.

'Go, Blossom! Go, Pippa!' Stardust called, as Blossom raced ahead.

Only the tops of the rocks were visible now. Blossom raced across the glistening, wet beach and into the sea, her steps slowing as the water deepened.

'Careful,' Pippa said, feeling Blossom strain against the current.

'Look!' cried Blossom. 'The horse-shoe!'

It was upside down, wedged between two rocks.

Just then a large wave crashed into Blossom, making her stumble.

'Eeek!' Pippa shrieked, as the wave soaked her too.

'Sorry,' said Blossom.

The seabed was uneven and covered in slippery seaweed. Pippa was amazed at how sure-footed Blossom was as she waded on.

'Don't ever let anyone tell you that you're clumsy,' Pippa told her.

'I'm not now, am I?' Blossom said delightedly. 'It's because I'm really concentrating and I'm not worrying that everyone is watching and laughing at me.'

When they were just an arm's length away from the rocks, Blossom suddenly stopped and wavered.

'Oh, horseflies!' she exclaimed. 'The current's too strong. This is as close as I can get!'

Chapter 7

Pippa stared at the rocks. Beneath her, the water swirled and bubbled like a giant's cooking pot. If she fell off Blossom trying to reach the horseshoe she'd never be able to swim against the current.

I'm not going to fall, she told herself. But Blossom's legs were buckling against the force of the whirlpool.

'Blossom, can you stand very still while I climb up your neck?'

'Yes,' said Blossom, 'but hurry! The tide's coming in really fast and I can feel the whirlpool sucking at my legs.'

Pippa quickly pulled herself towards Blossom's head. She clutched Blossom's mane with one hand and leaned over to the rocks. If only she could stretch a little bit further . . . Growing red in the face, Pippa reached out until her fingers were brushing the horseshoe. It was almost in her grasp.

Almost.

But the horseshoe was wedged firmly between the rocks and just couldn't be pulled free.

'Please hurry,' Blossom said urgently.

It was no good. The task needed two hands. Reluctantly, Pippa let go of

Blossom's mane and tried again. The horseshoe budged by the tiniest amount then stuck fast. Carefully, Pippa wriggled it backwards and forwards. It reminded her of wobbling a loose tooth. She rocked the horse-shoe forwards and backwards, until it shifted a bit more.

'Hurry!' whinnied Blossom.

The water was still rising and was splashing around Pippa's bare feet now. She yanked the horseshoe as hard as she could.

Over the roar of the whirlpool, Pippa thought she could hear Stardust calling her name from the shore. It made her feel braver to know that her best friend was cheering her on.

With all of her might, she pulled at the horseshoe again. She felt it grate against the rock then, suddenly, the golden horseshoe became free. The suddenness took her by surprise, and she slid backward, almost losing her balance. Wildly, Pippa grabbed Blossom's mane. As she did so, the horseshoe slipped through her fingers.

'No!' Pippa snatched at it, trapping it against Blossom's neck and only just preventing it from dropping into the churning water.

'I caught it!' she yelled.

Straight away Blossom swung round to face the beach and then froze in her tracks. Standing in the water a few hooves away were two scruffy ponies.

'Night Mares!' Pippa gasped, recognising Eclipse and Nightshade from the previous day and realising that they were the ponies she had seen at the edge of the Wild Forest.

'Give that back,' Eclipse said in a mean, shrill voice.

'It belongs to us,' said Nightshade.

The water was rising even higher by this point, and Pippa worried that they'd all be carried out to sea.

'PIPPA!' Stardust called from the beach.

Stardust's cry gave Pippa an idea.

'This horseshoe belongs on the

Whispering Wall,' said Pippa. Then she shouted to Stardust, 'Catch!'

Pippa hurled the horseshoe into the air and Stardust galloped to catch it in her mouth.

'NO!' cried Eclipse.

'Let's get out of here,' Pippa said to Blossom.

Blossom waded back towards the beach, and Pippa turned to see Night-shade and Eclipse still standing in the water, staring up at the headland. Pippa followed their gaze to see the mysterious cloaked pony looking down at them. The two Night Mares were just standing, as if glued to the spot, in the rising water.

'You two!' Pippa called, as Blossom

pushed further towards the shore. 'Get out of the water – it's dangerous!'

Pippa felt Blossom's muscles contract as she bravely fought against the tide. One careful hoof at a time, she waded back to the beach. Clutching Blossom's mane tightly, Pippa cheered her on until, at last, they were back on dry sand.

'That was close,' said Blossom.

'Too close,' agreed Pippa.

Stardust trotted up to Blossom and Pippa and gave the horseshoe to Pippa to hold.

'I tried to call to you,' she said. 'Those Night Mares came out of nowhere.'

'They were watching us,' said Pippa. 'And there was someone else watching too.'

'Who?' asked Stardust.

Pippa pointed to the top of the cliff, but the cloaked pony had vanished. She then turned to check on the Night Mares in the water – they were soggy and defeated, but wading clumsily through the shallows.

'I don't know,' admitted Pippa. 'But I

do know that we should get this horse-shoe back where it belongs – on the Whispering Wall!'

Stardust darted alongside Blossom and, side by side, they raced across the beach, leaving the Night Mares behind.

Pippa looked back to see the Night Mares emerge from the water. They started to come after Pippa and her friends, but the gap was too big for them to catch up. With an angry toss of their heads, they turned and galloped away in the opposite direction.

Blossom and Stardust began to climb the steep cliff path.

'You did it!' Stardust said, her dark eyes shining with happiness.

'We all did it,' said Pippa. 'Together!'

'I'm glad I have two best friends,' said Stardust.

'Look,' Blossom cried suddenly. 'The giant seahorses are watching.'

Pippa proudly waved the golden horseshoe above her head. The seahorses reared up in delight. Droplets of water flew from their spiky manes, falling like silvery fountains. Pippa sighed happily as she prepared to slide from Blossom's back.

'Don't get down yet,' said Blossom. 'I don't feel tired now.'

'What about the race?' Pippa asked. 'Don't you want to go back and finish it and get a medal?'

Blossom shook her head. 'There's always next year. I'll definitely enter the Equestriathon again, but right now I've got something that's much more important than a medal – two best friends.'

'Best friends for ever!' said Stardust.

'For ever,' Pippa and Blossom agreed.

Slowly, they went back up the path, stopping to pick up Pippa's sandals.

'Oh, I don't even remember dropping them,' said Pippa. 'I'll have to go barefoot. They're no good to wear.'

'Don't worry, the royal blacksmith will fix them for you,' said Stardust.

Triumphantly, they made their way back to the Royal Games grounds on the Plateau. It was impossible to keep the horseshoe a secret. When they approached the show arena a crowd of ponies quickly gathered to greet and cheer them. Pippa blushed deep red as some of the bolder ponies reached out to touch her with their noses as she passed.

The Queen and King were in the royal box watching the end of the Equestriathon. Pippa slid from

Blossom's back as Stardust led the way in. Quick as a flash, Cinders came out of her own box to block Blossom from following them.

'Only members of the Royal Court are allowed in here,' she said nastily.

But the Queen had already seen that

Pippa was carrying a horseshoe and she excitedly waved Blossom in.

'It's not fair,' Cinders hissed to her mother, Baroness Divine.

Divine narrowed her eyes. 'Good things come to those who wait,' she whispered back.

Pippa wondered why Baroness Divine never had anything nice to say, especially now, when they'd found another of the missing horseshoes. She soon forgot the Baroness, though, as she dropped a curtsy to Queen Moonshine. The Queen was the most beautiful pony she'd ever seen. Her golden coat seemed to glow and her pure white tail fell elegantly to the ground.

The Queen's face lit up with joy.

'The second missing horseshoe,' she whinnied. 'That's wonderful news. I'm very proud of you all.'

King Firestar stamped his hoof in agreement. 'We must put the horseshoe straight back where it belongs,' he said gravely.

A look of worry crossed the Queen's face. 'But it's almost time to award the prizes.'

'Stardust and her friends have proved themselves trustworthy and reliable. They could take the horseshoe back,' King Firestar suggested.

'Yes, please do,' the Queen replied.

Pippa was secretly pleased. There was something special about the golden horseshoe. Holding it gave her a tingling feeling that made her think the magic was rubbing off on to her somehow. It gave her courage.

When they reached Stableside Castle's courtyard, Pippa stood up on Blossom's back and carefully hung the horseshoe on the ancient stone wall. The three friends stood back to admire it as it sparkled prettily in the late afternoon sun.

'Two horseshoes are safe,' Stardust sighed, staring up at them in wonder.

'Our quest isn't over yet,' said Pippa. 'There are still six to find.'

'You've done enough for one day, child,' the King said, striding into the Royal Courtyard, accompanied by two ponies, with gleaming chestnut coats, who Pippa didn't recognise.

'Mum and Dad!' said Blossom.

'I thought you were staying to award the prizes?' Stardust said to her dad.

'When a father is proud of his daughter,' said the King, 'he ought to tell her.'

'And that goes for show ponies too,'

boomed Blossom's dad. 'You made your mum and me very proud today. We never realised how fast you were. If you want to carry on racing instead of doing dressage then you have our full support.'

Blossom beamed with delight. 'Thank you,' she whinnied.

'Now let's go back to the Games grounds,' said the King. 'You three deserve to have some fun — and we've got the evening's entertainment ahead.'

'A banquet, dancing and a huge fire-work display to end with,' Stardust said happily.

'Oh, I love fireworks!' said Pippa.

☆

Long troughs had been put up in the main arena of the Royal Games grounds and serving ponies were filling them with crunchy toffee apples, sugar-toasted oats and linseed-dipped carrots. Music was playing, coloured disco lights were flashing and lots of ponies were dancing together.

The three best friends ducked under the rosette-decked horseshoe arch but as they started for the arena Pippa heard someone shout, 'They're back!'

At once the music stopped and the disco lights went out. The dancers stilled and the crowd fell silent. Pippa flushed as all eyes turned towards her, Stardust and Blossom. The Queen was in the royal box and she beckoned them forward.

'Your determination and courage has resulted in another horseshoe hanging back where it belongs,' Queen Moonshine said in a clear voice. 'The Royal Ponies and the ponies of Chevalia thank you. Blossom, you have shown yourself to be a true friend of Chevalia. By putting the island's needs before your own, you missed out on winning a prize in the Equestriathon. For your courage and true selflessness you deserve a special award. Step forward.'

Nervously, Blossom did so. The Queen smiled as she placed a glittering tiara on her head. The sparkling gemstones were designed as a blue rosette, like a flower in blossom.

'To Chevalia,' said the Queen.

'To Chevalia,' cheered everyone, with Pippa, Stardust and Blossom cheering the loudest.

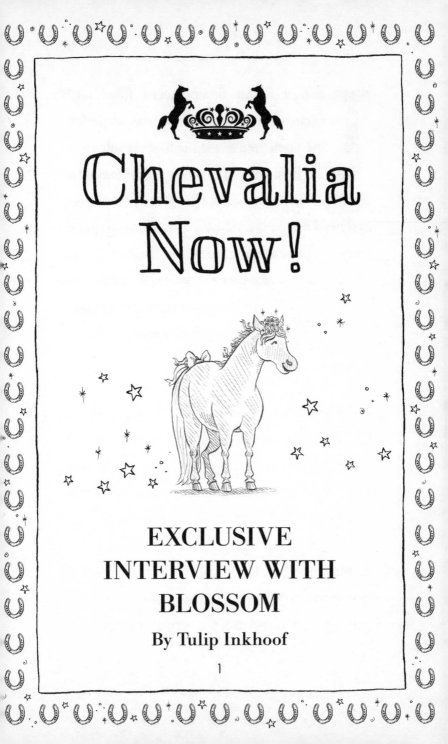

Chevalia Now!

EXCLUSIVE INTERVIEW WITH BLOSSOM

By Tulip Inkhoof

Today's Royal Games were filled with excitement and Blossom was definitely the pony who made the biggest splash. Reporter Tulip Inkhoof caught up with Blossom at the Royal Games grounds after Queen Moonshine bestowed a very special award on this very special pony at the evening celebrations. Read on for an exclusive interview with the dressage-competitor-turned-Equestriathon-racer . . .

☆ **TI (Tulip Inkhoof):** Blossom, this has been a big day for you. When you woke up this morning in your stable, did you have any idea that you'd become the pony of the Games?

☆ **B (Blossom):** To be honest, I just wanted to get through the dressage event – I was so nervous and I get clumsy when I'm nervous.

☆ **TI:** Was your dressage performance the low point of your day?

☆ **B:** Yes, unfortunately. You see, everyone in my family is an amazing show pony, but I've never been very good at dressage.

☆ **TI:** Yet you surprised everyone with your incredible performance at the Equestriathon. You're obviously built for speed!

☆ **B:** Well, I've always loved galloping. Sometimes after school I just like to go for a long gallop across the Savannah or along the beach. But it wasn't until my friend Pippa suggested that I enter the Equestriathon that I even considered putting my love of galloping to good use.

3

☆ **TI:** Oh yes, we must talk about Pippa. You're very lucky to have the human girl as a friend – the island is just buzzing about her! So, what's she like?

☆ **B:** Pippa's lovely and kind. She has a big heart and is full of courage.

☆ **TI:** Speaking of friends, you've been best friends with Princess Stardust for a really long time, but I understand that this friendship was put to the test today?

☆ **B:** Yes, Stardust has been my best friend for ages so I felt sad when she called Pippa her best friend, but today I learned that having two best friends can be twice as much fun!

☆ **TI:** You made a big sacrifice for your friends today – you had the lead position in the Equestriathon and yet you gave it up to race down to the beach. Can you tell our readers about it?

☆ **B:** I wanted to win that Equestriathon so badly, but when I saw my two best friends in trouble in the water nothing else mattered. I galloped down to the beach, where Stardust and Pippa were struggling to retrieve a golden horseshoe that was stuck in the rocks. The tide was rising around the rocks so it was very dangerous.

☆ **TI:** How did you feel?

☆ **B:** I was scared, but mostly I was scared that if I didn't do something then my friends would be in even greater danger. I realised that a lot of responsibility comes with being a best friend – you have to look out for one another. I may not have won the race, but I think I won something much more special – true friendship.

☆ **TI:** What's next for you?

☆ **B:** Right now I'm looking forward to dancing the night away with Pippa, Stardust and all the ponies who are celebrating the Royal Games. After the closing entertainment tonight, I'm going to start training for next year's Equestriathon. With the help of my friends, I might just win it!

☆ **TI:** I wish you the best of luck, Blossom, and enjoy your evening!

☆ **B:** Thank you, Tulip. By the way have you tried the toffee apples here? They're delicious!

BRINGING IN THE HARVEST

By Tulip Inkhoof

Tomorrow is Harvest Day on Chevalia! Harvest Day, famous for its mud and muck, is a long-standing tradition where everyone helps to bring in the harvest. All year long, the farm ponies have been hard at work, tending the Grasslands and vegetable plots. Harvest Day is their time to shine!

I spoke to hunky farmer pony Mucker and his older brother, Trojan, about their lives on the farm.

☆ **TI (Tulip Inkhoof):** Trojan, what's the best part of being a farm pony?

☆ **T (Trojan):** Well, Tulip, for me it's the sense of accomplishment when you see – and eventually eat! – the fruits of your labour.

☆ **M (Mucker):** You mean, the fruits, vegetables, grass and hay of your labour!

☆ **T:** Good one, Mucker!

☆ **TI:** What about you then, Mucker? As the youngest pony on the farm, what do you like best?

☆ **M:** My favourite thing is sharing the work with my friends, like Princess Stardust.

☆ **TI:** A Princess Pony on the farm? Surely you're joking!

☆ **M:** Not at all, Tulip. Stardust and I have been friends since we were foals and she loves to help out on the farm. We always have a lot of fun together.

☆ **TI:** Doesn't Stardust worry about her hoof polish getting chipped?

☆ **M:** Stardust may seem prim and proper in the Royal Court, but she's actually very adventurous and loves getting stuck in on the farm.

Well, readers, you learn something new every day! I can't wait to see the Royal Ponies get mucky on Harvest Day.

Be sure to check back tomorrow for my report on all the gossip from the farm!

Don't miss Pippa and Princess Stardust's
next adventure as they search for the
missing golden horseshoes on
Harvest Day!

Can they uncover another magical
horseshoe to save Chevalia?

Find out! In . . .

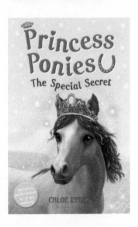

Turn over to read a taster

With Stardust's help Pippa had already found two horseshoes but now there were just four days until Midsummer and six horseshoes were still missing.

Putting the comb down, Pippa stood back to admire her work.

'Can we search the Horseshoe Hills today?' she asked.

'But it's Harvest Day,' Stardust said,

studying her reflection in a long mirror. 'Everyone who attends Canter's Prep School of Fine Equine is expected to go to the Grasslands to bring the harvest home. That includes me.'

'Oh!' Pippa's heart sank.

Even though Chevalia was under threat, Stardust's parents, Queen Moonshine and King Firestar, were determined that the Royal Family continued their many traditions and kept up appearances so as not to worry everyone.

'Harvest Day is fun,' Stardust assured her. 'And it's not all work. The best bit is the picnic lunch — it's rather like a party with all our favourite things to eat, like carrots dipped in linseed oil.'

'I suppose we haven't searched the Grasslands yet,' mused Pippa.

'Then we'll do it today while we're helping with the harvest,' Stardust said decisively.

Pippa wasn't sure how much searching they would have time for if they were expected to work but it was better than nothing.

'Let's go then,' she said, eager to get started.

After a hurried breakfast in the Castle's huge dining room Pippa, Stardust and the four of her brothers and sisters who still attended Canter's Prep School followed their nanny,

Mrs Steeplechase, down to the Grass-lands.

'Stop it,' Pippa whispered, trying not to giggle as Stardust imitated the way her teacher waddled.

'No talking!' Mrs Steeplechase said, spinning round to glare at them.

'Sorry,' said Pippa. She turned her

attention to the lines of ponies who were approaching the Grasslands from every direction. They were lots of foals, their manes and tails braided with purple ribbons, trotting beside their parents.

'They're from Canter's Nursery School,' Stardust explained. 'The infants wear purple ribbons, while the juniors wear red ribbons like me, and the seniors wear blue ones. We should have plaited red ribbons in your hair too. When we get to the Grasslands I'll ask if anyone has any spare so you're not left out.'

'Thanks,' Pippa said absently, her mind on the missing horseshoes. She really hoped that they would find at least one today . . .